Nothing was more exciting than fighting dragons
or finding treasure – but then he rode h

Even the bravest princes get lonely sometimes.

So Prince Percy went to his parents.
"I want to get married," he said.
"Be careful," they warned him.

"You'll be miserable unless you marry a **REAL** princess,
someone who loves you for **YOU**, not for your treasure."

The question is, how can you tell if you've found
a REAL princess?

Why, you ask the cleverest inventors in the kingdom to help.

The inventors worked under swirling, curling clouds of smoke. Potions bubbled and tiaras twinkled as they tinkered away. Eventually one jumped up. "EUREKA! I've got it!" she cried.

The inventor took Percy to the biggest, grandest, tallest room in the palace and stopped beside an enormous white sheet.

The sheet was pulled back to reveal
a bed – a very tall bed with a

tottering,
teetering
tower
of mattresses.

"Nothing escapes the notice of a **REAL** princess," explained the inventor.

"**I**f she can feel something tiny, like this little pea, through all these pillow-soft mattresses, she'll pass the real princess test."

From Titicaca to Timbuktu,
every princess in the world was
invited to take the test.

The king and queen sent
their fastest messengers
to seek them out.

Princess Map

PRINCESS
WANTED

Within days, carriage after carriage pulled up. The palace became very lively indeed as it filled with princesses.

The princesses
pranced and they
danced, they laughed
and they larked...

...but they didn't seem very interested in Percy.

One by one, the princesses
took the test...

...and one by one they slept
right through the night.

When they woke up,
no one mentioned a pea.

So, one by one, Percy sent them away, until the palace was quiet again.

The following night, during a thundering storm, Percy heard a

KNOCK!

KNOCK!

KNOCK!

on the door.

Out of the rain stepped
a shivering stranger.
"May I shelter here
tonight?" she pleaded.

"Of course!" Percy said
to the dripping-wet girl.
"My palace is always
open to those in need."

They sat by the toasty-warm fire, sharing adventure stories, until Percy couldn't keep his eyes open.

The next morning, Percy woke up beside the dying fire... alone.

But then...

...the girl walked in.

"Good morning, sleepy head!" she said.

"Where have you been?" Percy asked.

"After you fell asleep, I looked for a bed – and I found one, as tall as a house!"

"And... how did you sleep?" whispered Percy.

"Well the bed looked so soft..." She yawned. "But I just couldn't get comfortable."

Percy gasped. "Are you a REAL princess?"

"How did you know?" she gulped.

Percy took her to see the pea, explaining
the inventor's test on the way.

The girl laughed. "You've been seeking your real
princess while I've been seeking my perfect prince!"

"I promised to marry any prince who was kind enough to take in a stranger. I've walked from palace to palace. You're the only one who let me in."

They married to the sound of bells and birdsong.
And so began the rest of their blissfully happy –
and adventurous – lives together.

Years later, they opened a grand museum for the trinkets and treasures they had found. At its heart, they placed their lucky pea under a crystal dome.

It may still be there today.

'The Princess and the Pea' was written by Hans Christian Andersen in 1835. The son of a shoemaker and a washerwoman, he became one of the most famous fairy tale writers in the world.

Edited by Lesley Sims

Designed by Laura Nelson Norris

First published in 2018 by Usborne Publishing Ltd., Usborne House, 83-85 Saffron Hill, London EC1N 8RT, England. www.usborne.com Copyright © 2018, 2017 Usborne Publishing Ltd.